THE KINGFISHER BOOK OF
Fairy Tales

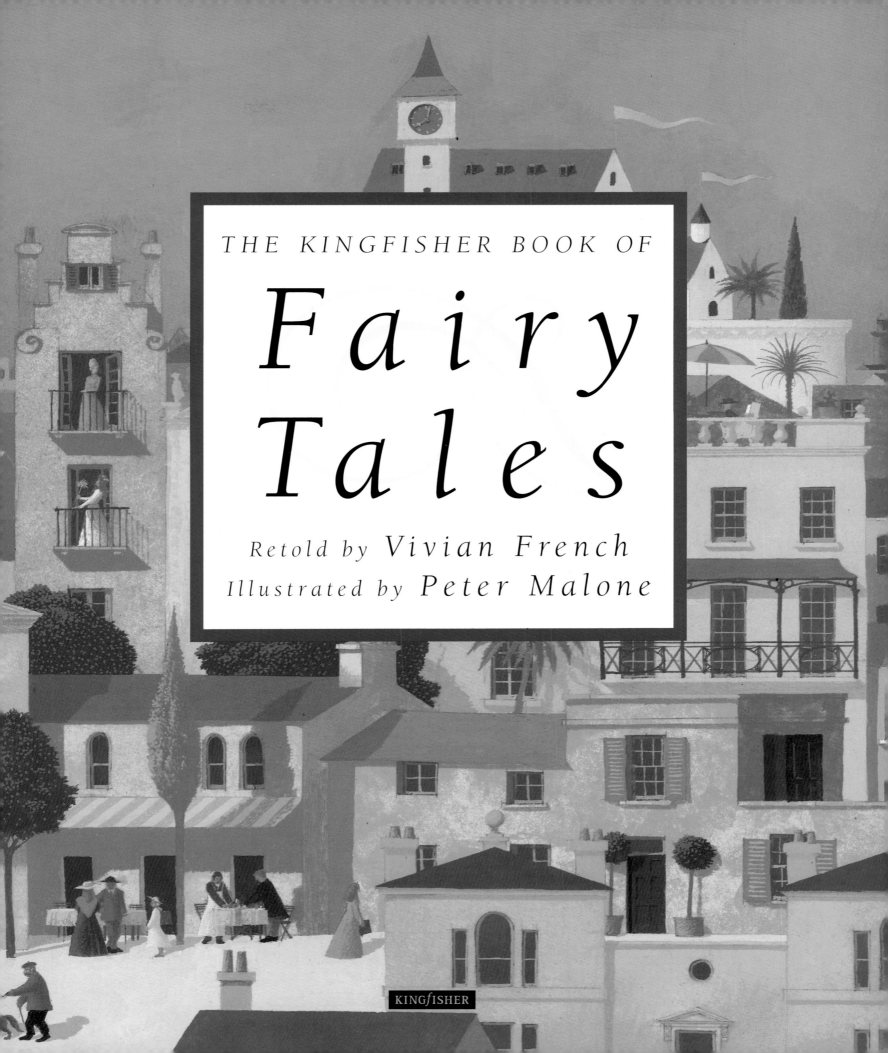

THE KINGFISHER BOOK OF

Fairy Tales

Retold by Vivian French
Illustrated by Peter Malone

KINGFISHER

For Ann-Janine & Richard
V. F.

For Helen
P. M.

KINGFISHER
An imprint of Kingfisher Publications Plc
New Penderel House, 283-288 High Holborn, London WC1V 7HZ

First published in hardback by Kingfisher 2000
2 4 6 8 10 9 7 5 3 1
1TR/0700/GC/GC/157MA

A CIP catalogue record for this book is available from the British Library.

ISBN 0 7534 0394 3

Designed by Ian Butterworth
Printed in Hong Kong

Contents

Foreword

*"CINDERELLA – YOU **SHALL** GO TO THE BALL . . ."*

The very first time my dad read me the story of Cinderella something burst into flower inside me. That promise wasn't only for Cinderella – it was for me, too. I was small and ordinary and often considered myself overlooked in favour of my siblings . . . but suddenly there was the possibility of magic in the air. I was enchanted by fairy tales, and I've remained so ever since.

When deciding which of these tales to retell, I was looking for that touch of magic – a sense of enchantment, of some mysterious force that changes the ordinary into the extraordinary. There had to be something other than simple endeavour – this, it seems to me, is the distinguishing factor separating "fairy" from folk tales. I wanted every child reading these stories to feel that sudden sparkle just as I did, to believe that even in our modern world of analysis and fact, anything is possible.

So as source material I went back to the tales of my childhood: the brothers Grimm, Jacobs, and also Perrault. In addition I read and re-read any versions of the stories that I could find, from a seventh century Chinese Cinderella onwards. I do not claim to offer a faithful interpretation of any one ancient or modern retelling; I have retold these seven tales as I would tell them to any child that I know and love.

I loved <u>listening</u> to fairy tales long before I could read them for myself: with this in mind I rejected the complex in favour of a clear and lineal narrative. I tried to write in such a way that both younger listeners and older readers would find the stories accessible and immediate.

Within these seven tales I was determined to include as many traditional "fairy" elements as possible. I wanted promises, wishes, transformations; a giant, a witch, elves – and, of course, a fairy godmother. I looked for stories where heroes and heroines rise from unhappy and humble origins to happiness and riches – such as when Cinderella, the poor ill-treated youngest daughter, goes to the ball and wins the love of a prince. Hope is a wonderful message to offer children. In "Hansel and Gretel", a boy and a girl without mother or home still defeat the wicked witch and return to their father with riches enough to change their lives forever.

There are stories here that look at help and promises. The shoemaker and his wife are duly grateful and do not abuse the fairy help they are given. The fisherman's wife, on the other hand, asks for too much – with the result that she has to be taught a lesson. Fairy power is certainly not without problems: "Rumpelstiltskin" could easily have ended in tragedy if the miller's daughter had not had human help – but hard work and love wins through and arrogance loses. Even if you are young and foolish like Jack (and the despair of your mother), risks can still pay off – as long as you are agile enough to beat the giant to the bottom of the beanstalk.

The setting of the stories was also a consideration: hearthside ashes and royal palaces; moonlight shining as Hansel and Gretel walk hand-in-hand under the dark pine trees; waves rocking the boat as the fisherman rows out to sea; the land beyond the clouds at the top of the beanstalk; the everyday interior of a shoemaker's shop;

the mysterious world of Rumplestiltskin as he dances in the darkness, lit only by the flickering flames of his fire . . . Each story has its own particular landscape, time and place. Peter Malone took this to his heart. I am breathless at the way in which he has created seven fairy tale worlds that are somehow all entirely different and wonderfully beautiful, but each holding that sense of the fantastical in the ordinary, the possible in the impossible – that is real magic.

There is a dark side to every tale, but surely it is true to say that without darkness the light can never shine. Children <u>are</u> frightened by shadows and bats and bogles . . . fairy tales recognize this fear. A diet of bland happiness and undiluted sweetness refuses to acknowledge that such fears are valid. Isn't this much more frightening than a frank admission of the existence of giants of one sort or another – together with firm proof that they can be outwitted and defeated? A child will always identify with the hero or heroine and will, therefore, overcome difficulties in a blaze of triumph just like Jack . . . or Beauty . . . or Hansel and Gretel.

Fairy tales are, surely, the most magical place for a child to go exploring. I believe that these seven tales offer a sufficiently wide variety of theme and enchantment to whet the appetite of young readers for many, many more such tales . . . so they may, indeed, read happily ever after.

June 2000

Jack and
the Beanstalk

Once upon a time there was a boy, and his name was Jack. He wasn't very clever but he didn't mind. He was quite happy sitting on a fence singing, "*Dee-dah diddle-di-dee.*"

Jack and his mother lived in a tiny cottage with a cat and an old brown cow called Daisy. Jack's father had died when Jack was a baby, and since then Jack and his mother had always been very poor. Jack's mother told him they had once had gold and silver and other fine things, but Jack took no notice of her tales. He just sat on a stool and sang, "*Dee-dah diddle-di-dee.*"

Jack's mother took in other people's washing to make a little money, but as she got older she found this harder and harder. Jack was no help to her. He dropped the washing and lost the pegs and forgot to look to see if it was raining. He was much too busy sitting on the doorstep singing, "*Dee-dah diddle-di-dee.*"

At last there was no money left at all.

"Jack," said his mother, and there were tears in her eyes, "Jack! You must take poor Daisy to market and sell her. Sell her for as much money as you can, for we have nothing left."

Jack grumbled a little, but his mother pushed him out of the door. She led the cow out of the field and gave Jack the rope. "Take care, Jack," she said. "Make sure you hurry back from market, and keep the money safely in your pocket."

Jack nodded and set off down the road. He sang, "*Dee-dah diddle-di-dee,*" as he went.

Jack and Daisy had not gone far when they saw a man striding along towards them. His coat was red, his trousers were blue and his scarf was a brilliant yellow. Jack stopped to stare.

"Good morning, young sir," said the man. "That's a fine cow you've got there. I don't suppose you'd be wanting to sell her?"

Jack nodded. "I'm taking her to market."

"Fancy that," said the man, "fancy that. Now, I can tell you're a clever lad. How about you selling me your cow, and I'll give you something you'll never get in the market. I'll give you this bag of magic beans!"

Jack stared at the little bag. Magic beans! What could be better than magic beans? He took the bag and gave the man Daisy's rope, and then he ran all the way home as fast as he could to tell his mother how clever he had been.

Jack's mother didn't think he had been clever at all.

"Beans?" she gasped. "You sold our cow for BEANS? You silly SILLY boy!" And she snatched the beans and threw them out of the window. "GO TO BED AT ONCE!"

Jack went slowly up the stairs to bed, and his mother sat down to cry and worry.

TAP! TAP! TAP!

Jack woke up with a start. Something was tapping on his bedroom window. He yawned and stretched and climbed out of bed. He went to the window . . . and his eyes opened wider than they had ever opened before.

"OH!" he said. "It's a BEANSTALK!" and he flung on his clothes and rushed outside to look.

The beanstalk went up and up and up. "It goes up to the clouds," Jack said, "but where does it go after that?" And he began to climb.

Up and up and up Jack went, until his house looked like a toy below him. Up and up and up he climbed, until the clouds swirled around him and he could hardly see. Up and up and up he clambered – until suddenly the clouds were beneath him and he found himself standing in a strange bare land. In front of him was a long winding path, and far away at the end of the path was a huge grey castle.

"*Dee-dah diddle-di-dee,*" Jack sang as he walked along, but as he got nearer to the castle he stopped singing. The chimney was as tall as a tower. The windows were enormous. The front doorstep was higher than Jack's waist.

Jack took a deep breath and heaved himself up, but the doorbell was way above his head. He picked up a stone and hammered on the door.

CREEEEEEEEEEEEEEEEAAAAAAAAAAAAAAK!

The door opened, and Jack looked up. A giantess looked down.

"Oh, what a dear little boy!" she said. "But you mustn't stay here! Hurry away, or my horrible brother will eat you all up!"

Jack leant against the door. "I'm SO hungry," he said.

"Oh, dearie dearie me," said the giantess. "Well . . . he won't be back for a while. Come in, you poor little thing."

The giantess walked into her kitchen, and Jack followed her. She picked him up, and sat him on a jam jar with a saucepan for his table. Then she gave him bread and soup, and Jack ate until he could eat no more.

THUMP! THUMP! THUMP!

The kitchen shook. "Oh, dearie me!" said the giantess. "If it isn't my brother home early! Quick, little boy! HIDE!" And she picked Jack up and popped him inside a cupboard.

Inside the cupboard Jack held his breath. He heard the giant thundering down the hall. He found a crack and peeped out — and nearly fell off his shelf. The giantess was big, but the giant was enormous. His head touched the ceiling as he stood in the middle of the kitchen and sniffed.

"FEE FI FO FUM
I SMELL THE BLOOD OF AN ENGLISHMAN!
BE HE ALIVE OR BE HE DEAD
I'LL GRIND HIS BONES TO MAKE MY BREAD!"

"Now, now," said the giantess. "That's only your dinner you can smell. Sit you down, and I'll put it on the table."

The giant grumbled, but he sat down. Jack watched in wonder as the giant gobbled and gulped a mountain of meat pie and slurped and burped a sea of gravy. When he had finished he banged his massive fist on the table and shouted out:

"BRING ME MY GOLD!

BRING ME MY HEN!

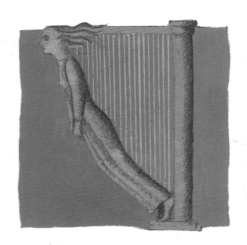

BRING ME MY HARP!"

The giantess hurried to a chest in the corner. She threw open the lid and brought out a bag of gold, a fine fat hen and a golden harp. She put them on the table next to the giant. He never said thank you.

"BE OFF WITH YOU!" he roared. "I WANT TO BE ALONE!" And the giantess crept out of the kitchen.

Clink! Clink! Clink! The giant carefully counted the gold pieces out of the bag and back into the bag. Then he pointed to the hen.

"LAY!" The hen gave a squawk, and laid an egg of solid gold. The giant nodded and put the egg in his pocket. He pointed to the harp.

"PLAY!"

"Dee-dah diddle-di-dee," sang the harp.

Jack's mouth fell wide open. The harp was playing his song! How could it know that tune? Jack shook his head in wonder.

"Dee-dah diddle-di-dee." The harp went on playing, and the giant's eyes slowly closed. His head sank down onto the table, and he began to snore. Jack silently pushed open the cupboard door.

It wasn't easy for Jack to climb the table leg. Twice he nearly fell, but he hung on tightly and at last he was at the top. The giant was snoring steadily, and the hen and the harp were sleeping too. Carefully, carefully, Jack picked up the bag of gold. Carefully, carefully, he slid down the table leg with the bag on his back. Carefully, carefully, he tiptoed across the kitchen floor and down the long hall to the front door. Then, as soon as his feet were fairly on the path, he ran all the way back to the beanstalk.

WHEEEEEEEEEEE!

WHEEE EEEEEEE!

Jack slid down the beanstalk and landed at the bottom with a bump. His mother was so pleased to see him safely back home, she never said a word about the beans or the beanstalk. When he showed her the bag of gold she threw her arms around him.

"Jack!" she said. "You are a clever CLEVER boy! Why, your father had a bag of gold just like this one, but long long ago it was stolen away."

"Maybe this is my father's gold," said Jack.

His mother shook her head. "No no, Jack," she said. "How would your father's gold be found at the top of a beanstalk?"

21

For seven weeks and seven days Jack stayed at home with his mother, but he thought about the beanstalk all the time. He thought about the hen and the golden eggs. He thought about the harp and how it played, "*Dee-dah diddle-di-dee.*" At last he told his mother he was going to climb the beanstalk again, and although she begged him not to, he said he had to go.

Up and up and up Jack went, just as he had before. Through the clouds he went, just as he had before, up and up and onto the path. He hurried to the castle and knocked on the door, but this time the giantess did not want to let him in.

"A dear little boy like you came once before," she said, "and he took my brother's gold. My brother is not a good man, and he was very very angry. If he sees you he will swallow you down in one big gulp!"

"PLEASE let me in," Jack begged, and the giantess opened the door. She gave him bread and meat, and when the giant came home she popped Jack in the cupboard.

"FEE FI FO FUM
I SMELL THE BLOOD OF AN ENGLISHMAN!
BE HE ALIVE OR BE HE DEAD
I'LL GRIND HIS BONES TO MAKE MY BREAD!"

roared the giant, but the giantess patted his arm and told him to sit down and eat. Jack watched and waited, and when the harp had played, "*Dee-dah diddle-di-dee, dee-dah diddle-di-dee,*" and the giant was fast asleep, he scrambled up the table leg, just the way he had before. He crept across the table top, tucked the sleeping hen under his arm, slid down to the floor . . . and ran. As he reached the top of the beanstalk he heard a terrible shout from far far away: **"WHERE'S MY HEN?"**

Jack's mother could not believe how clever he was when he came home with the hen.

"A hen that lays golden eggs!" she said. "Why, your father had a hen just like this one, but long long ago it was stolen away."

"Maybe this is my father's hen," said Jack.

His mother shook her head. "No no, Jack," she said. "How would your father's hen be found at the top of a beanstalk?"

"SQUAWK!" said the hen, and laid a golden egg.

Jack's mother smiled and smiled. "We'll be rich forever and ever! You'll not need to go up that nasty beanstalk any more."

Jack shook his head. "Just one last time, Mother," he said.

And although his mother begged and begged him not to go, he did. The song of the golden harp floated in his head and he could not forget it. As he climbed up and up and up he sang, "*Dee-dah diddle-di-dee.*"

It took Jack a long time to persuade the giantess to let him in. She said her brother never stayed away for long now, and that he was always sniffing and snuffling in the hope of finding the little boys who had stolen his gold and his hen. But at last she agreed to give Jack something to eat and took him into her kitchen.

Everything happened as it had before, but this time the giant ROARED into the kitchen shouting:

"FEE FI FO FUM
I SMELL THE BLOOD OF AN ENGLISHMAN!
BE HE ALIVE OR BE HE DEAD
I'LL GRIND HIS BONES TO MAKE MY BREAD!"

"Hush, brother," said the giantess. "It's the meat pie you can smell," but the giant sniffled and snuffled round and round the kitchen while Jack trembled in the cupboard.

At last the giant settled down to eat his mountainous meal, but even as he ate he stopped to sniff and snuffle. The giantess brought him the golden harp, but still the giant was restless.

"*Dee-dah diddle-di-dee,*" the harp played over and over again, but the giant did not sleep.

Jack watched and watched and waited and waited, until the giant's head sank down at last and his snores filled the room. At once, Jack slipped out of the cupboard. It took him no time to reach the top of the table, and he snatched up the harp and slung it over his shoulder.

"*DEE-DAH DIDDLE-DI-DEE!*" sang the harp.

The giant reared up. Jack tumbled down to the floor and ran. The giant lumbered to his feet. When he saw that the harp was gone he let out such a roar that the castle trembled, and Jack staggered as he ran.

"COME BACK HERE!" bellowed the giant, "AND I'LL GRIND YOUR BONES TO MAKE MY BREAD!"

Up the hall and out of the door Jack panted, and the giant thundered after him. Along the path he puffed, and leapt onto the beanstalk, the giant close behind him now. The beanstalk shuddered and swayed as the giant began to climb down after Jack.

"MOTHER! MOTHER!" Jack yelled as he slithered faster and faster towards the ground. "MOTHER! QUICK! BRING AN AXE!"

Jack's mother came hurrying out of the house. When she saw the giant looming large above her she screamed and ran to fetch the axe. Jack leapt down, grabbed the axe and began to hack at the beanstalk as hard as he could. There was a creaking . . . and a groaning . . . until –

CRASH! The beanstalk fell, and the giant fell with it. The ground cracked open, and the giant disappeared forever.

Jack and his mother stared at each other.

"Phew!" said Jack.

"Goodness me!" said his mother.

"*Dee-dah diddle-di-dee!*" sang the harp on Jack's shoulder.

"OH!" said Jack's mother, and she clutched Jack's arm. "Jack! Jack! Wherever did you find that golden harp?"

Jack put the harp on the ground. "At the top of the beanstalk, Mother," he said.

"Why, your father had a golden harp just like that," his mother said, "and it played that very same tune. When you were a very little boy it played you to sleep every night. It MUST be your father's harp! And you've found it!"

Jack smiled proudly.

"*Dee-dah diddle-di-dee,*" he sang, and the harp sang with him.

"*Dee-dah diddle-di-dee. Oh, how happy we'll be!*"

And they were.

Hansel and Gretel

Long ago and far away there was a forest of tall green pine trees that whispered all day long. At the edge of the forest was a small house, and in the house lived a widowed woodcutter and his two children, Hansel and Gretel. Their clothes were thin and ragged and they often did not have as much to eat as they would have liked, but they were happy together.

When Hansel and Gretel were still quite young their father married again. The children tried to make their stepmother welcome, but she did not care for them. She moaned and groaned about how little money their father earned, and how little food there was to go round.

"If there were only two of us," she said to the woodcutter, "think how much more we'd have!"

The woodcutter shook his head, but his new wife took no notice. "Children are so greedy," she said. "We should take them out into the forest and leave them there. I'm sure they'd find plenty to eat."

The woodcutter did not want to leave his children because he loved them very much. But his wife did not, and she was clever. Every night she whispered to him how much happier Hansel and Gretel would be in the forest.

"There are roots and mushrooms and wild honey from the bees," she told him. "You can see how thin and skinny the children are now. If they lived in the woods they'd soon be as fat as butter!"

It was true that Hansel and Gretel were thin and skinny, and as time went on they grew thinner and skinnier. The woodcutter didn't know that the stepmother was eating most of the food he brought home. He began to think that she was right, and that his children would find more to eat in the woods.

"Tomorrow we will take my little ones into the forest and leave them there," he said, and he sighed. "I only hope that the oak and the ash and the holly trees will take better care of them than I can."

The woodcutter did not see Hansel and Gretel in the corner of the room, listening.

When the children went to bed that night Gretel began to cry.

"Don't cry, Gretel," said Hansel. "I know what to do!" And he tiptoed down the stairs and out of the house. Quickly he filled his pockets with white pebbles from the path and hurried back to bed.

The woodcutter and his wife woke Hansel and Gretel very early in the morning.

"We have a long way to go today," said the woodcutter, and he looked very sad.

"Hurry up! Hurry up!" said his wife.

Off into the forest they walked, but Hansel walked a little behind his father and stepmother and sister.

"Stop dawdling!" snapped the stepmother.

"I'm only looking at our little white duck swimming in the river," said Hansel.

"There's no time for that," said the stepmother. "Hurry along!" She did not see him dropping the pebbles behind him, one by one by one.

The woodcutter and his wife took Hansel and Gretel deeper into the forest than they had ever been before.

"Now," said their father, "you must be tired. I will build a little fire to keep you warm and you can rest. Here is a piece of bread; eat it when you are hungry."

The stepmother caught the woodcutter's arm. "Come," she said, "we have work to do."

Hansel and Gretel sat down. They were very tired and, although they meant to stay awake, their eyes closed.

When they woke up it was dark and they were quite alone.

"Oh, Hansel!" said Gretel. "Whatever shall we do?"

"Just wait until the moon comes up," said Hansel.

When the moon swam into the dark sky the forest turned to silver and Hansel's white pebbles shone out. The children laughed and skipped as they followed the pebbles all the way back home.

The woodcutter was surprised and very pleased when Hansel and Gretel came knocking on the front door. His wife was not, but she was clever.

"You see?" she said. "They are well able to look after themselves. Tomorrow you must take them even further into the forest." She looked out and saw the pebbles gleaming in the moonlight.

"H'm," she said to herself. "So that's the way it was!"

When Hansel came tiptoeing down the stairs later that night to fetch more pebbles, he found the door was locked. The key was in the stepmother's pocket.

Early the next morning the woodcutter woke Hansel and Gretel.

"Hurry and get ready," he said, and he gave them each a small piece of bread. "Don't eat it too soon, my little ones. We have a long way to go."

Once again they walked deeper and deeper into the forest, and Hansel walked a little way behind his father and sister.

"Hansel, what are you doing?" his father asked.

"I'm only looking at a little white dove on the top of the pine tree," Hansel said, but he was crumbling his bread in his pocket and tossing the crumbs behind him, one by one by one.

"Will we be able to find our way home?" Gretel whispered, and Hansel nodded.

Once again their father made them a little fire to keep them warm. Once again they slept, tired out by their long walk. Once again when they woke it was dark and they were quite alone. The stars were shining and the moon was creeping out behind the clouds.

Gretel sat up and stretched. "Shall we go home now?" she asked.

Hansel did not answer. He was looking all around, his heart beating fast. There was no sign of the trail of bread. While he and Gretel had been sleeping, birds had fluttered down and eaten every crumb.

Hansel and Gretel wandered this way and that all night long, but they could not find their way out of the forest. When the sun came up they were still lost, and very lonely too.

"I'm so tired," Gretel said. "Will we ever get home?"

"Of course we will," said Hansel. "Look! There's a little white dove! It keeps looking at us. Do you think it's the same little dove that I saw before?"

"Let's follow it," said Gretel.

The children walked on, and the dove flew in front of them. Suddenly Hansel rubbed his eyes.

"I think I can see smoke!" he said.

"Yes! Yes! I can see a roof!" said Gretel.

"THERE'S A HOUSE!" they shouted together, and they began to run helter-skelter through the trees.

When Hansel and Gretel reached the house they stopped and stared.

"Oh!" they said. "OH! OH! OH!" For the house was made of crispy golden gingerbread, with soft sweet cake for the roof and shining sugar windows.

"I'm SO hungry," said Hansel, and he broke off a piece of gingerbread and gave it to Gretel. He tore off another piece for himself.

"Nibble nibble nibble!" said an old cracketty voice. "Who's that nibbling at my little house?"

Hansel and Gretel stared. Out of the house hobbled a bent and twisted old woman with sharp little eyes.

"Oh," said Hansel. "We're so sorry—"

"But we were VERY hungry!" said Gretel.

The old woman smiled at them. It was not a nice smile, and her eyes looked sharper than ever. Gretel moved closer to Hansel and he took her hand.

"You poor little dears," the old woman said. "Why don't you come inside?"

Hansel looked at Gretel, but Gretel shook her head.

The old woman put her hand on Hansel's shoulder. "I'll give you barley broth and good white bread," she said, and indeed a delicious smell was floating out of the house.

Hansel looked at Gretel and licked his lips.

Gretel looked at Hansel and nodded.

The bent old woman led Hansel and Gretel inside the gingerbread house. A little table was spread with a pretty cloth, and on the table were two bowls full to the brim with hot barley broth. "Here, my little dears. Come and sit down!" And the old woman pushed them towards two little chairs.

The broth was the best that either child had ever tasted, and so was the bread. Gretel had three helpings, and Hansel had four. When they had finished the old woman showed them to two little beds.

"Come and sleep, my little dears," she said, and Hansel and Gretel thanked her as they lay down. Their eyes closed, and they slept.

Early the next morning the old woman shook Gretel awake. "Quick, girl, quick! Get out of bed! There's work to do!" and she pulled at Gretel's arm. Gretel sat up and stretched.

"Where's Hansel?" she asked when she saw his empty bed.

"Safe and sound, safe and sound," said the old woman, and she pointed her long, bony finger to a dark corner. In the corner was a small cage, and inside the cage was Hansel.

"Let him out! Let him out!" Gretel ran to Hansel's cage and tugged at the bars.

The old woman laughed her cackling laugh. "Tee hee, my little dear. Your brother is skinny enough just now – but he'll make a fine dinner for me when he's fattened up!" And she dragged Gretel away.

"I know what you are!" Hansel shouted. "You're a witch! Let my sister go!"

But the witch just cackled again.

All day and every day the witch kept Gretel working. She made her chop the wood, carry the water, weed the garden and scrub the floors. Most of all Gretel had to cook and cook and cook. Sweet sugar buns and crunchy chocolate biscuits, tarts dripping with sticky treacle and cakes bursting with fat black currants and ruby red cherries . . . all of these were fed to Hansel. All the witch gave Gretel was a bowl of the thinnest soup and a piece of dry bread.

Every evening the witch went to Hansel's cage and asked him to put his finger out between the bars so she could feel how fat he was getting. But Hansel was clever. He found a little stick and stuck that out instead. The old witch did not see very well, and every time she felt the twig she muttered, "Skinny as a stick! Still skinny as a stick!"

At last the witch could wait no longer. She felt Hansel's twig, and she stamped her foot. "Fat or not, I'll eat you now!" she said, and she called for Gretel. "Build up the fire! Pile up the sticks! Heat the oven hotter than it's ever been before!"

Gretel trembled as she did as she was told. She brought more and more sticks, and the flames rushed and roared up the chimney.

"Is the oven hot?" asked the witch, and she licked her lips.

"Very hot," said Gretel.

The witch rubbed her bony hands together. "Open the door and peep in to see," she said, but Gretel shook her head.

"I don't know how."

"Foolish girl!" snapped the witch, who was meaning to push Gretel right in and cook her first. "How can you be so silly? Watch! Do it like this!" And she opened the oven door and peeped right in . . . and Gretel ran at her from behind and gave her one huge push. Into the oven went the witch, and CLANG! the door slammed shut behind her. The flames went blue, and the flames went green, and POOF! . . . that was the end of the witch forever and ever.

"HURRAH!" called Hansel. "HURRAH!"

Gretel ran to open his cage and set him free. Together the children ran round the house, looking in every box and basket. They found gold and silver, and diamonds and rubies, and filled their pockets to the very top. Then they took a handful of cake from the roof and set off to find their way home.

It wasn't difficult for Hansel and Gretel to find their way as the white dove flew in and out of the trees in front of them. At last they came to a river, and on the other side they could see the path that led to their very own house.

"How shall we cross the river?" asked Gretel.

"Look!" said Hansel. "There's our little white duck! Why don't we ask it to carry us across?"

"Two of us together will be too heavy," said Gretel.

"So it will," said Hansel. "Little duck, little duck, may we take turns to ride on your back?"

The duck carried the two children across the river, first Gretel and then Hansel.

"Thank you, thank you!" said Gretel, and she gave the duck the last of the cake from the gingerbread house.

"Hurry!" said Hansel. "Let's run!"

He took Gretel by the hand, and they ran and ran along the path to their very own house.

"Father! Father!" they called. "We're home!"

Their father hugged them and kissed them and cried with happiness. "I've missed you," he told them, "I missed you every hour of every day."

The stepmother was not at home. She had tired of the woodcutter and gone away to the town, never to return, and no one was sorry that she had gone.

When the woodcutter saw the treasure that Hansel and Gretel had found he could hardly believe his eyes.

"Now, dear Father," said Gretel, "we can live happily ever after."

"So we can," her father said, and Hansel threw his hat in the air and shouted,

"HURRAH!"

The Fisherman and His Wife

At the sandy edge of the Great North Sea was a pigsty. No pigs had lived in it for a long long time, for it was very small and damp, and any pig who saw it said, "OINK! OINK!" and ran away. Only a poor fisherman and his wife lived there, and that was because they had nowhere else to live.

Every day the fisherman went out to fish, and every day his wife waved him goodbye and wished him luck.

SLIP SLAP, SLIP SLAP, SLIP SLAP . . . The fisherman rowed his little wooden boat out to sea. He spread his nets on the rocking waves, and sat and waited all day long before he pulled them in again. Sometimes he caught nothing, and sometimes he caught a crab or two, and sometimes his net was full of silvery leaping fish. At the end of the day he would row back home, *SLIP SLAP, SLIP SLAP, SLIP SLAP*. If there were no fish he and his wife had no supper, but on the good days he and his wife ate well and were happy.

As time went on there were more and more bad days when the fisherman caught nothing. Perhaps the summer was too hot and too long, or perhaps the fish had swum far away . . . the fisherman couldn't tell. He grew hungry, and his wife grew cross.

"Come along, Fisherman," she said, "you can't be trying." And she sent him out earlier and earlier in the morning, until one day she woke him even before the sun had risen. "Hurry along, hurry along!" she said, and the fisherman walked slowly down the shore to his boat.

SLIP SLAP, SLIP SLAP, SLIP SLAP . . . The fisherman pulled on his oars, and the little wooden boat skipped along the top of the waves. The sun began to warm the day, and the fisherman yawned as he tossed out his nets, and sat back to wait. He leant on his oar to watch the sun glinting on the water, and his eyes began to close.

SPLASH! The fisherman woke with a start. Something was thrashing about in his net. He hurried to pull it in, and saw a huge silver fish with a golden crown caught in the tangled ropes.

"Goodness me!" said the fisherman, "what's this? It must be the king of all the fishes! How beautiful it is!" And as quickly as he could he untied the knots and let the fish go free.

"Thank you, Fisherman," said the fish. "Thank you. If you ever have need of me, call for the King of Fishes!" And he leapt in the air and dived back into the sea, and the water drops sparkled like diamonds.

The fisherman bundled his net into the boat and rowed for the shore as fast as he could go. *SLIPETTY SLAPETTY, SLAPETTY SLAPETTY, SLIP SLAP SLIP!*

"Wife! Wife!" he called as he ran up the sand. His wife came hurrying out to meet him.

"Why are you home so early? Is the net full of fish?"

"No, no!" said the fisherman. "The net is empty! But I've seen something wonderful – I've seen the King of Fishes!" And he told his wife about the wonderful silver fish.

"H'm," said his wife. "King of the Fishes, was he? And you let him go? Without asking him for anything in return?"

"I didn't want a reward," said the fisherman. "It was enough to see such a beautiful thing."

"That's as may be for you," said his wife. "But what about me, and what I might want? You're a foolish man, Fisherman, you really are. A fish like that is magic, and magic means

wishes, and wishes mean good things for the two of us. You get back in your boat and find that fish. Tell him we want our wish – we don't want to live in a dirty old pigsty any more. You tell him we want a cottage, a proper little cottage with roses at the door and pretty curtains at the window. Now – be off with you!"

SLIP . . . SLAP, SLIP . . . SLAP . . . The fisherman rowed slowly. He did not know what he should say to the King of Fishes. He stared at the blue-green sea and whispered, "King of Fishes in the sea, if you hear me – come to me."

SPLASH! The fisherman looked up. The King of Fishes was swimming beside the little wooden boat.

"What do you want, Fisherman?" he asked.

The fisherman shook his head. "I'm sorry to bother you, Your Majesty," he said, "but my wife thought you might be kind enough to grant us a wish . . ."

"What does she want?" asked the fish.

"A little cottage," said the fisherman, "with roses at the door. Oh, and pretty curtains at the window."

"It is done," said the King of Fishes, and he sank away out of sight.

The fisherman looked across the sea. Sure enough, there on the edge of the sand was the prettiest little cottage he had ever seen. There were roses at the door, and spotted blue-and-white curtains flapping at the windows. A curl of smoke drifted out of the chimney, and the fisherman's wife was standing at the door waving to him.

"She'll be happy now," said the fisherman, and he rowed back home.

The fisherman's wife was indeed happy. She was very happy for one week, and quite happy for another week . . . but in the third week she began to grumble.

"You're a foolish man, Fisherman, you really are," she said. "When that fish gave you a wish you should have asked for a house, not a silly little cottage. Why, there's hardly room to move here – and the roses are covered in thorns. Get back in your boat, and go and find that fish. This time make sure you ask him for something better. I want to live in a great big house, and I want a flag flying on the roof, and a coach and six white horses at the door."

SLIP . . . SLAP, SLIP . . . The fisherman rowed slowly, slowly. The sea was grey and cold around him, and cross little waves snapped at his oars. The fisherman sighed heavily, and said, very softly, "King of Fishes in the sea, if it please you – come to me."

SPLASH! There was a swirling of water, and the King of Fishes was beside him.

"What do you want now, Fisherman?" he asked.

"Oh, Your Majesty," said the fisherman. "I am truly sorry, but my wife is still not happy. She wants a great big house, a great big house with a flag flying on the roof . . . and a coach and six white horses at the door."

"It is done," said the King of Fishes, and he sank away out of sight.

The fisherman looked across the sea. Sure enough, there on the edge of the sand was the finest house he had ever seen. Five red-and-yellow flags were flying from the rooftop, and a gold coach and six white horses were standing outside the wide front door. The fisherman's wife was standing at a window, and she nodded her head as the fisherman rowed back home.

The fisherman's wife was very happy with the house for a week, and quite happy for another week . . . but in the third week she began to grumble.

"You're a foolish man, Fisherman, you really are," she said. "Sometimes I think you have no sense, no sense at all. Can't you see that a house is MUCH too small for a fine woman like me? And all those flags flapping about by day and by night. It's too bad, indeed it is. You get straight back in that boat of yours and tell that fish I want something better. I want a palace, that's what I want. And while you're at it, tell him I want to be queen. And he might as well make sure that everybody bows when I ride by. Now, be off with you, and be quick about it."

SLIP . . . SLAP . . . The fisherman rowed slowly, slowly, slowly. The sky was dark, and the wind was blowing the waves into angry rollers that crashed onto the shore. The fisherman's little wooden boat tossed and twisted over the stormy water, and he held tightly to his oars as he called out, "King of Fishes in the sea, please, I beg you – come to me."

SPLASH! There was the King of Fishes, his silver scales flashing amongst the heaving waves.

"What is it now, Fisherman?" he asked.

"It's my wife," said the fisherman, and his voice trembled as he spoke. "Now she wants a palace, and she wants to be queen . . . and she wants everyone to bow as she rides by."

"It is done," said the King of Fishes, and he sank away out of sight.

The day was too dark and the waves were too high for the fisherman to see the land. He turned his boat and rowed home, pushed and buffeted by the angry sea. As he dragged his boat up the sand he saw a mighty palace towering above him, and a soldier in silver armour waiting for him.

"The queen will see you when you are dry," said the soldier. "She does not wish you to walk in the palace with wet and dirty feet. You are to bow when you meet her, and you must call her Your Majesty."

The fisherman was so surprised that he could only nod and follow the soldier into the palace.

The fisherman's wife was sitting on a throne when the fisherman came in to see her. She was wearing a long red satin cloak, and a crown glittering with diamonds. The fisherman stared at her and forgot to bow. "Goodness me, Wife!" he said. "You DO look grand!"

The fisherman's wife was very happy with her palace for a week. She was quite happy for another week . . . but in the third week she began to grumble.

"Fisherman," she said, "I've been thinking."

"Have you, Wife?" said the fisherman.

"Yes," said his wife. "It's all very well being queen, but what can I do that other queens can't?"

"Well," said the fisherman, "everybody bows to you. And you can order people you don't like to be sent to the dungeons."

"I want something better than that," said his wife. "I want to be queen of more than a few miserable men and women and children. I want to be queen of the whole world . . . and I want to be queen of the sun and the moon and the stars!"

"Oh, Wife!" said the fisherman. "No one can be queen of the sun and the moon!"

His wife jumped up from her throne. "I can! And I will! Go down to the shore and get in your boat and ask that fish! Ask him NOW! Tell him I want to be queen of the sun and the moon and the stars, and I want the sun to rise when I want and to set when I want! Go! Go! GO!" And she pushed the fisherman out of the door.

The fisherman walked slowly and heavily down to the sandy shore and climbed into his little wooden boat. The sky was black with thunderclouds, and the water boiled and churned as a furious wind raged over the angry sea. The fisherman could hardly row; he was tossed and tumbled from wave to wave, and he clutched at the sides of his boat in fear.

"King of Fishes in the sea, if you hear this – pity me!"

If there was a splash the fisherman never heard it, for at that moment the storm broke over his head. Lightning flashed, and thunder roared and rolled across the purple storm clouds. The fisherman crouched down in his boat, and above him the waves towered up and up . . . and even taller than the waves was the King of Fishes.

"WHAT DO YOU WANT, FISHERMAN?" he demanded, and his voice was louder than the thunder.

The fisherman shivered and shook at the bottom of his boat.

"My wife . . ." he whispered, "my wife . . . she would be queen of the sun and the moon and the stars . . ."

"GO BACK TO THE SHORE, FISHERMAN!" The voice of the King of Fishes rolled over the waves as they crashed about the little wooden boat. "GO BACK, AND SEE WHAT YOU WILL SEE!"

One last huge wave caught the fisherman's boat and threw it high in the air. The terrified fisherman shut his eyes tightly, and waited for the sea to close about him . . . but instead he was swept in a roaring green glassy fist of water all the way to the top of the beach.

The fisherman opened his eyes. Sure enough, there he was, in his boat on the sandy shore he knew so well. Below him the sea still ranted and raged, and the wind blew cold about him. He climbed out of the boat . . . and stared.

There was no palace. There was no house. There was no cottage. There, as it had been for years and years, was the pigsty. And running out of it, her arms outstretched, was his wife.

"Oh, FISHERMAN!" she said as she hugged him tightly. "I thought you must surely have drowned in that storm . . . and it would have been all my fault! Oh, Fisherman – whatever have I done?"

The fisherman scratched his head as he looked at the pigsty.

"Well, Wife," he said, "it seems to me that nothing very much has changed. We lived in a pigsty once, and now we live in a pigsty again."

The fisherman's wife patted his arm. "But I've changed, Fisherman," she said.

"Have you, Wife?" asked the fisherman.

"Yes," said his wife.

And when the fisherman next went out in his boat, his wife was there beside him to heave on the net and to pull on the oars.

SLIP SLAP, SLIP SLAP, SLIP SLAP . . .

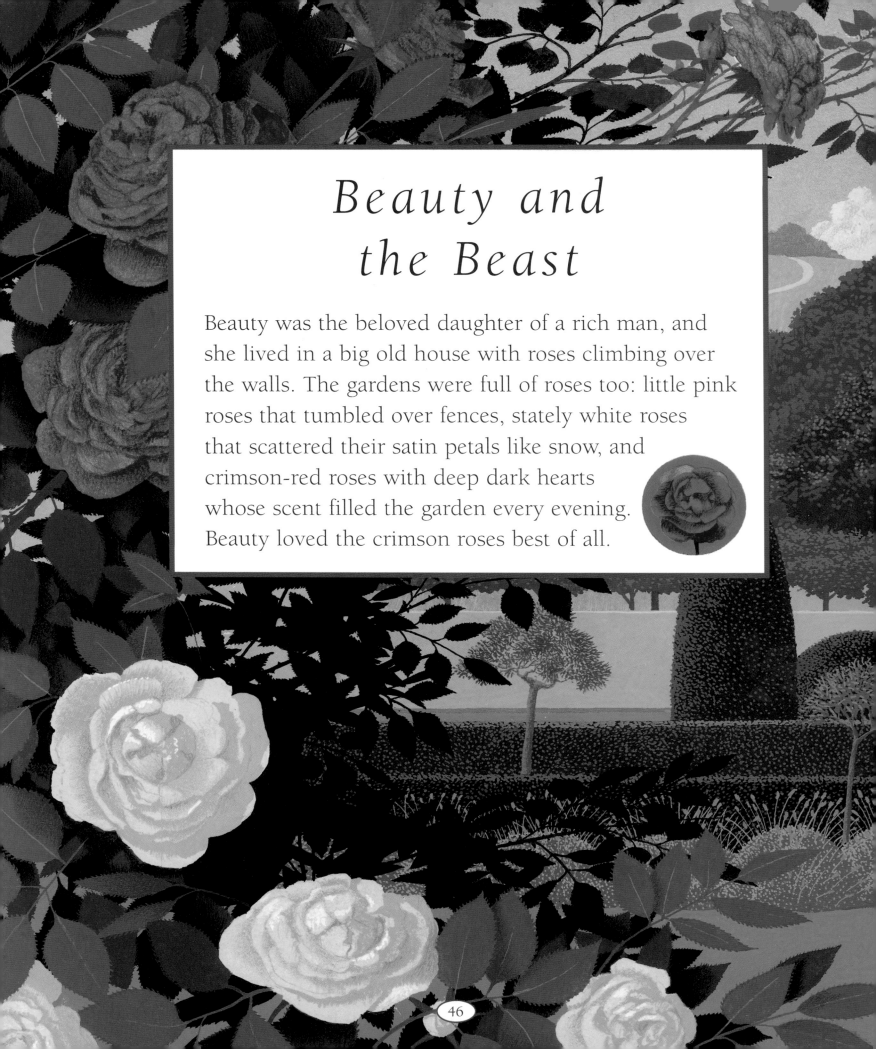

Beauty and the Beast

Beauty was the beloved daughter of a rich man, and she lived in a big old house with roses climbing over the walls. The gardens were full of roses too: little pink roses that tumbled over fences, stately white roses that scattered their satin petals like snow, and crimson-red roses with deep dark hearts whose scent filled the garden every evening. Beauty loved the crimson roses best of all.

One terrible day the rich man lost all his money. All his ships were wrecked in a storm, and he had nothing left. He called for his seven sons and seven daughters, and he told them that they must leave the big old house and go and live in a tiny tumbledown cottage. The seven sons and six of the daughters wept and wailed and stamped their feet, but Beauty went to her father and kissed him.

"Poor Father," she said.

Now there was no money, the sons and daughters all had to work. They grumbled and muttered amongst themselves – all except for Beauty. She sang as she scrubbed the floors and fetched the water and peeled the potatoes. Her brothers and sisters looked at her and sneered. "What's the point of singing when there's nothing to sing about?" they said.

Exactly a year after he had lost all his money, Beauty's father heard that one of his ships had been found.

"I must hurry to the city," he said. "A little of my fortune may be saved!"

His sons and daughters danced with joy.

"Bring us back velvet suits," said the sons.

"Bring us satin dresses!" said the six daughters.

"I will, I will," promised their father. "And would you like a satin dress too, Beauty?"

Beauty shook her head. "I do so miss the roses," she said. "Dear Father – please will you pick me a rose?"

Her brothers and sisters laughed at her, but her father nodded and rode away.

Beauty's father was away a long time. He learned there was no money left, and no hope of any more to come. At last he began to make his way home, riding on his tired old horse.

The wind blew colder and colder as he rode along, and it began to snow. The snow grew deeper, and the old horse stumbled as she walked. At last she stopped, and Beauty's father looked around him.

"Brrrrr! It's so cold and dark! Where am I?" He slid off the horse's back and stared into the whirling snow. Suddenly he stepped forward. "Look, old horse! A light! I can see a light!"

Beauty's father and the old horse hurried as fast as they could go. They found the light was shining from the windows of a castle, and as they got closer they saw the gates were wide open.

In the castle yard a stable was ready for the old horse with fresh straw and water. As Beauty's father staggered towards the massive castle door, it opened and a wonderful smell of bubbling stew and roasting potatoes floated out.

Inside the castle Beauty's father stood and stared. There was a warm fire, a hot meal, a comfortable bed – but there was no sign of any human being.

"Is anybody here?" he called, but there was no answer. Only an echo answered, "Here . . . here . . . here . . ."

Beauty's father shook his head. "I'm so tired and hungry," he said. "I wonder if I dare take just a little to eat?"

"Eat . . . eat . . . eat . . ." replied the echo, and Beauty's father sat down at the table.

As he finished his meal, Beauty's father saw the plates floating away exactly as if they were carried by invisible helpers. He rubbed his eyes and looked again, but he couldn't see anyone. "This must be a magic castle!" he said as he took himself off to bed.

In the morning Beauty's father woke up to find that his clothes were clean and dry, and hot chocolate and fresh white rolls were ready on the table. "This is a truly magical place," he said to himself. "I wish my dear Beauty could see it."

He went to the window to look out, and he saw that the sun was shining down on a garden of tangled roses – and every rose was crimson-red.

"Even if I have no money I can still pick a rose for Beauty," he said, and he hurried outside.

"GRRRRRRRRRRRRRRRR!"

As soon as Beauty's father picked the rose there was a terrible roaring and a huge and horrible beast rushed at him.

"THIEF!" it roared, "THIEF! How DARE you steal my roses? I shall lock you in my dungeons forever and ever and EVER!"

Beauty's father shook and shivered with fear. "Oh, sir," he said, "I didn't know – you have been very kind – indeed you have. I only picked the rose because Beauty loves them so very much."

"Beauty loves roses, does she?" growled the beast. "And who is Beauty?"

"My beloved daughter," said her father. "I have fourteen children, and I promised them velvets and satins, but I have no money. All Beauty wanted was a rose . . ."

"GRRRRRRR . . ." The beast began to prowl round and round Beauty's father. "GRRRRRRR . . . Suppose I let you go?"

Beauty's father fell on his knees. "Oh, sir – please do! Please let me go home to my children—"

"GRRRRRRRRRRRRRRRR!"

Beauty's father trembled as the beast roared again.

"SILENCE!" said the beast, "and I will let you go. I will give you gold and silver – but you MUST come back! You must come back and bring Beauty with you. And if she will stay here with me forever, you may go free. If she will not –" and the beast held up his sharp-clawed scaly paw – "then I will hunt you down wherever you are."

Beauty's father rode slowly away from the castle. He was carrying the bags of gold and silver, but his heart was very heavy. How could he ask Beauty to live with such a terrible beast?

"I know," he said. "I will take the gold and silver safely home and then go back to the beast alone." He shuddered. "He will be very angry – but at least Beauty will be safe."

Beauty was the first to see her father riding out from the forest. "Father!" she called, and she ran to hug and kiss him. All her brothers and sisters ran after her, and they seized the bags of gold and silver with shouts of joy.

Beauty looked at her father's unhappy face. "What is it, Father?" she asked. "Why are you so sad?"

Her father gave her the crimson-red rose. "Oh, dear Beauty," he said. "I can't stay . . ." and tears rolled down his cheeks.

His sons and daughters crowded round him. "Why?" "What is it?" "Why must you go?" they asked.

At first Beauty's father wouldn't say what was wrong, but at last he told them about the beast, and how he wanted Beauty to go and live in the castle. "But I shall go back alone," he said.

"There!" Beauty's brothers turned on her. "This is your fault!"

"That's right!" said her sisters. "If you hadn't asked for a rose none of this would have happened!"

Beauty took her father's hand. "Take me back with you," she said. "This beast can't be so terrible – after all, he did let you go."

The next day Beauty kissed her brothers and sisters goodbye and rode off through the forest with her father. They said very little to each other as they rode along. As they went up the steps to the castle door they held hands tightly.

"GRRRRRRRRRRRRRRRRR!"

The beast leapt into the hallway. His hair was long and tangled, and his teeth were very sharp. Beauty gave a little gasp as she looked at him. Her heart was pounding, but she took a deep breath and curtsied low.

"Good day, Beast," she said.

The beast growled a long low growl. "GRRRRRRR. Did you come of your own free will?"

"I did," said Beauty.

"And you will live here forever and ever?" asked the beast.

"I will," said Beauty.

"Good," said the beast, and he turned to Beauty's father. "Be gone!"

Beauty's father could hardly say goodbye to her, his eyes were so full of tears. He turned and hurried to his horse and rode away.

In the castle the beast led Beauty to a room full of sunshine and singing birds.

"Here," he said. "This is your room. You can go where you want, and take what you want. My servants will bring you what you need . . . but you will not see them."

Beauty curtsied. "Thank you," she said, and turned away to the window.

The beast did not leave the room. He stood staring at Beauty, his eyes burning under his shaggy hair.

"Beauty," he growled, "will you marry me?"

Beauty spun around. "Oh NO!" she said. "I can't do that!"

"GRRRRRRR!"

The beast gave a mighty roar, so loud that the windows rattled and the walls shook, and he rushed out of the room. Beauty shivered as she heard him snarling and stamping away, and she ran to shut and lock the door behind him.

That night Beauty did not sleep well. She heard growls and roars even in her dreams, and she dreamt she heard a voice calling, "Beauty! Beauty! See me! Help me!"

When Beauty woke in the morning she ran to the window, but all she could see was the garden full of roses.

Knock knock! It was a very small polite knock, and Beauty opened her door. She could see no one – but all of a sudden there was her breakfast on a little table. Her tea was poured and her bread was buttered for her, but she could see no one lifting the teapot or holding the knife. As she finished eating, a cupboard opened, and Beauty saw it was filled with pretty dresses and shoes – all exactly her size.

"Thank you," Beauty said to the empty room – and for a moment she thought she felt a soft touch on her cheek.

All that day Beauty wandered about the castle and the garden, but she was always alone. The invisible servants helped her find her way and brought her anything she wanted just as soon as she thought of it. It was only when she sat by her fire in the evening that she heard heavy footsteps coming up the stairs. Beauty began to tremble, but she told herself not to be so silly. "After all," she said, "why would he look after me so well if he wanted to harm me?" And when the beast came in to see her she thanked him and smiled at him as kindly as she could.

The beast's eyes gleamed. "Beauty," he said, "Beauty – will you marry me?"

Beauty shook her head. "No," she said. "I can only marry someone I love."

The beast roared loudly and rushed out of the room, but Beauty was not so frightened this time. It seemed to her the beast was not quite as angry as he had been the day before.

The days went by, one after another. Beauty wandered in the garden or explored the castle, and every day she found something new that pleased her. One day it was a lake covered with rose-pink water lilies, and another day it was a small stripey kitten curled up on her bed. There were pictures in every corridor of the castle, and Beauty saw that they changed every day – unless it was a picture she particularly liked. Her favourite foods were always served, and if ever she thought of something new – like raspberries and cream – it was sure to appear at the very next meal.

Music played as Beauty walked in and out of the rooms of the castle: soft music if she wanted to be quiet, or a foot-tapping tune if she wanted to dance. One day she discovered a library full of her favourite books, and she was surprised to learn the beast had read them all and liked them too.

Every evening the beast came to visit Beauty, and little by little she began to look forward to seeing him. Each night he asked her to marry him, but when she told him that it was not possible he no longer growled or rushed away. He would just sigh.

The only time Beauty was sad was when she thought of her dear father. One day the beast found her leaning against a window with tears in her eyes.

"What is it?" he asked, and his voice was gentle.

"If only I could see my father again," Beauty said. "I do miss him so much."

The beast shook his head. Beauty thought he, too, looked sad beneath his shaggy hair. "If I let you go, you will never come back," he said.

"Oh, dear Beast, I will! I promise!" Beauty jumped up. "May I go? I will come back — indeed I will!"

"Will you, Beauty?" said the beast. "I hope so. If you stay away I shall surely die."

Beauty was delighted to think she was going home. She packed trunks full of presents for her brothers and sisters and her father.

"How will I get home?" she asked the beast.

The beast sighed very heavily. "Take this ring," he said. "Put it on your finger tonight, and when you wake up you will be in your father's house. At the end of seven days put it on your finger again, and it will bring you back. Don't forget, dear Beauty. Seven days is all that I can bear. If you stay longer I will die."

"I promise," Beauty said.

That night Beauty hurried to her room and put the ring on her finger. When she woke up she was amazed to find herself in her own small bed at home, with her sisters unpacking the trunks beside her. They were pleased to see her again and so were her brothers — especially when they saw their presents. Her father was so happy he hugged her and hugged her and hugged her.

The seven days passed very quickly. Beauty walked and talked with her father. She went riding with her sisters, and danced with her brothers. She visited her neighbours and her friends, and laughed and played with them. She did not notice how the seven days had come and gone . . .

The eighth and ninth days went by, and Beauty was still at home. On the tenth night she had a dream. She dreamt she was walking by a lake, and she found the beast lying in the reeds. His fur was matted and tangled, and his eyes were closed. In her dream Beauty tried and tried to wake him, but he would not wake.

When morning came, Beauty ran to tell her father she must go back to the castle. "My poor Beast," she kept saying, "my poor Beast!" That night she said goodbye to her brothers and sisters and went to bed with the ring on her finger.

When Beauty woke it was still night-time, but she was back in the castle. She snatched up a shawl and ran out of her room.

"Beast!" she called. "Beast! Where are you? Oh, answer me – please!"

There was no answer.

Remembering her dream, Beauty ran out into the gardens. The moon shone brightly overhead as she hurried to the lake, and there – just as she had seen it in her dream – was the beast, lying very still amongst the reeds. His hair was matted and tangled, and his eyes were closed. Tears ran down Beauty's cheeks, but as she bent over him she saw he was still breathing.

"Beauty . . ." he whispered, "Beauty . . . I am dying."

"Oh, dearest Beast!" Beauty cried, and she threw her arms around his neck. "Don't die! Please don't die! Don't leave me – I love you so much!"

TANTARAAA! TANTARAAAA! TANTARAAAAA!

There was the sound of triumphant trumpets. All around Beauty and the beast stars burst into glittering showers of gold, and rose petals cascaded out of the sky until the ground was covered in scented crimson petals.

The beast shook himself, and stood up. "Close your eyes, Beauty," he said, and Beauty shut her eyes.

TANTARAAAAA!

The trumpets sounded again.

"NOW!" said the beast's voice, and Beauty opened her eyes. She saw a young and handsome prince, and as she stared at him he held out his hands.

"Dearest Beauty," he said, "don't you know me? You have broken the spell. Beauty — will you marry me?"

"OH!" said Beauty. "Oh . . . dear, dear Beast . . . but I would have loved you even as you were . . ." And she kissed him, and he kissed her too.

The wedding was the most wonderful wedding that anyone had ever seen. All Beauty's family came, and so did everyone from miles around. Kings and queens and princes and princesses filled the castle, and the trumpets played all day . . . and Beauty and her prince lived in peace forever and ever.

The Elves
and the Shoemaker

SNIP, SNIP, SNIP. STITCH, STITCH, STITCH. TAP! TAP! TAP!
The shoemaker's shop was very small, but very busy. All day long he
snipped and stitched and tapped as he made boots and shoes and
slippers. His wife swept and tidied round him and she sang as she
worked. They were happy together, and promised each other that the
shoes they sold would always be very good, and
very cheap. "We can't let men and women and
children go barefoot for the sake of a penny or
two," said the shoemaker, and his wife agreed.

SNIP, SNIP . . . STITCH, STITCH . . . TAP! TAP!

As the weeks and months and years went by the shoemaker and his wife grew older and poorer and hungrier. Their shop was small, and the people of the town forgot it was there and went to buy their boots and shoes at the big new town over the hill.

"Should we move to the big town ourselves?" asked the shoemaker's wife.

The shoemaker shook his head. "This is our home," he said, "and tomorrow is another day. Our shoes are very good and very cheap. I'm sure things will get better."

SNIP . . . STITCH . . . TAP!

Things did not get better. They got much worse, and at last there were no pennies left and nothing at all in the kitchen cupboard.

"I have just enough leather to make one last pair of shoes," the shoemaker said. "I will cut them tonight, and tomorrow I will make them."

"And after that?" said his wife.

The shoemaker patted her arm.

"Tomorrow is another day," he said. But neither he nor his wife slept very well that night.

BONG! BONG! BONG! BONG! BONG! BONG!

The church clock struck six and the shoemaker got up to make the last pair of shoes. He went sadly down the stairs to his shop – but he stopped in the doorway in amazement. There, on the table, was a wonderful pair of shoes, made from the leather he had cut out

the night before. The shoemaker rubbed his eyes, but the shoes did not disappear. He picked them up and took them to the window to look at them. They were perfectly made, with the tiniest of stitches. The shoemaker called for his wife, and she came hurrying in to stare as well.

BANG! BANG! BANG!

Someone was knocking at the door of the shop. The shoemaker's wife opened the door and a man in a suit of the finest velvet came striding in.

"Good morning! Good morning!" he said. "What a wonderful pair of shoes! They're exactly what I'm looking for! May I ask how much they cost?"

The shoemaker and his wife looked at each other. They didn't know what to say.

The man in the velvet suit pulled a purse from his pocket.

"Here!" he said. "Such a magnificent pair of shoes deserves a magnificent price!" And he handed the shoemaker the purse, took the shoes and strode out of the shop.

"Well I never!" said the shoemaker.

"Fancy that!" said his wife, and she emptied the purse onto the table. "Oh, Shoemaker! Look! So much money!"

JINGLE! JINGLE! JINGLE!

The shoemaker shook the purse as he walked along the road to the market. He had enough money to buy leather to make two pairs of shoes. There was even enough to buy bread and cheese.

That afternoon the shoemaker smiled as he cut out the leather, and his wife hummed as she swept up the cuttings and leavings.

"I'll make the shoes tomorrow morning," the shoemaker said. "Tonight we'll have a good supper!"

"Indeed we will," said his wife, and she gave the shoemaker a kiss.

BONG! BONG! BONG! BONG! BONG! BONG!
The shoemaker got up the next morning as the church clock struck. He went down the stairs to his shop – and again he stopped and stared. There, on the table, were two pairs of shoes. They were beautiful shoes, beautifully stitched – and made from the leather the shoemaker had cut out the night before.

"Wife!" called the shoemaker. "Wife! Quick! Come and see!" And his wife came hurrying in to stare.

BANG! BANG! BANG!
Someone was knocking at the door of the shop. The shoemaker's wife opened the door, and in came two grand ladies dressed in satins and silks.

"What delightful shoes!" they said, clapping their hands. "We must have them!" And they tossed a handful of gold coins onto the table, picked up the shoes, and sailed out onto the street.

"Well I never!" said the shoemaker.

"Fancy that!" said his wife, and she scooped up the coins and counted them out. "Shoemaker! Shoemaker! If this goes on we'll be eating supper every single night!"

JINGLE! JINGLE! JINGLE!
The shoemaker shook the coins in his pocket as he walked along the road to the market. He bought enough leather for four pairs of shoes, and meat and potatoes besides.

He sat in his shop that afternoon, cutting and cutting. His wife sang as she swept up the bits and pieces all around him. The shoemaker yawned as he put his scissors down.

"I'll make the shoes tomorrow," he said.

His wife gave him a hug. "Meat stew tonight," she said.

BONG! BONG! BONG! BONG! BONG! BONG!
The next morning the shoemaker found four pairs of
shoes on the table. As he peered at them, the old
shoemaker saw that each pair was stitched with the
same tiny stitches.

"They're better than anything I've ever made," he
said to his wife. "Why, there's not a single mistake.
They're perfect shoes!"

"So they are, my dear," said his wife, "but then
it was you that cut out the leather."

BANG! BANG! BANG!
When the shoemaker's wife opened the shop door there was a queue outside. The
four pairs of shoes were sold in minutes, and a heap of gold and silver coins left on
the table.

"Well I never!" said the shoemaker.

"Fancy that!" said his wife, and she poured the coins into the shoemaker's pockets.
"You'd better be off to the market, my dear. Perhaps you could buy me a new broom.
My old one is worn out." And she waved the shoemaker goodbye as he went on his way.

SNIP, SNIP, SNIP. SNIP, SNIP, SNIP.
From that day on the shoemaker and his wife became richer and richer. Every day the shoemaker carefully cut out the leather – eight, sixteen, thirty-two pairs – and the next morning he and his wife would find the finished boots or slippers neatly lined up on the table. Their fame spread, and once again the men and women and children of the town came to buy – and so did the people from the big town over the hill.

BANG! BANG! BANG!
Every morning the queue at the shoemaker's door grew longer. It was very nearly Christmas and everyone was wanting new shoes. The shoemaker was as busy as he had ever been, and his wife sang all day long. One afternoon, however, she stopped and leant on her broom.

"Shoemaker," she said, "I've been thinking. All these months someone has been helping us. Someone has been stitching and sewing the shoes we sell, and they've never had a penny or a thank you. Why don't we watch and see who it is?"

The shoemaker put down his scissors. "You're right, Wife," he said. "We'll watch tonight."

TIPTOE, TIPTOE, TIPTOE.
That night the shoemaker and his wife crept into the shop and hid themselves behind an old curtain. The pieces of leather for the next day's shoes were on the table, just as usual.

"I wonder who will come?" whispered the shoemaker.

"Shh!" said his wife. She had heard a little noise.

PATTER, PATTER, PATTER!
As the shoemaker and his wife peeped around the curtain, two little elves came skipping into the room. They hopped up onto the table and sat stitching and sewing the whole night long. The shoemaker and his wife watched with wide eyes. As the morning sun came beaming through the window, the elves yawned, stretched and hopped off the table and away. Every last shoe was finished, stitched and sewn to perfection.

"WELL I NEVER!" said the shoemaker.

"FANCY THAT!" said his wife. "And the poor little things wearing nothing but rags!"

The shoemaker stood up, and picked up one of the shoes.

"Those little elves have done a lot for us, Wife," he said. "It's right that we should thank them. If you will make them shirts and trousers, I will make them shoes and belts to match."

His wife agreed at once and went to fetch her sewing needles. She cut up a handkerchief of finest lawn and made two tiny shirts. She used pieces of green and red velvet to make two tiny pairs of trousers and two tiny jackets. She found a wisp of the softest lamb's wool and knitted two pairs of snow-white stockings.

The shoemaker hunted through the box of scraps for the thinnest, silkiest leather he could find. He made two little belts of leather, and two tiny pairs of bright red boots. He spent all day stitching them with the tiniest of stitches, until at last they were ready. The shoemaker put them on the table with the clothes, and then, as soon as it was dark, he and his wife hid once more.

PATTER, PATTER, PATTER! The two elves came skipping and scampering into the shop. Up onto the table they hopped – and then stopped and stared.

"Trousers of velvet! And jackets! And boots!" they called out, and their voices were as small and as high as a bat's whistle. They clapped their hands and laughed and pulled on the clothes as fast as they could. When they were quite dressed they pranced and danced and bowed to each other.

"So fine we are, so fine are we, that gentlemen we both will be!" they said. And they bowed once more, jumped off the table and danced away.

The shoemaker and his wife never saw the elves again. The shoemaker made boots and shoes and slippers all by himself, but now his stitching was as small and neat as that of the elves. His wife went on singing as she swept. Good luck stayed with them and there was always a queue outside the shoemaker's shop.

SNIP, SNIP, SNIP. STITCH, STITCH, STITCH. TAP! TAP! TAP!
The shoemaker's shop was very small, but it was very busy . . .

Rumpelstiltskin

Once there was a miller who had a daughter, and very proud of her he was too. He boasted about her to everyone he met, and some of his stories were true – and some were not.

"She's as beautiful as the sun!" said the miller. "She's as wise as the owl in the deep dark woods!" Then one day he told a woman that his daughter was so clever she could spin straw into gold. The woman told her husband and the husband told a soldier and the soldier told the king.

"A girl who can spin straw into gold?" said the king. "Why, that would be an excellent thing for me and my kingdom! We have fields and fields of straw, but not so much as a bag of gold. With gold I could buy myself a big stone castle and a crimson velvet cloak . . . and everyone in the kingdom could have their very own cottage and their very own pig. Tell this girl to come to my palace at once!"

The miller jumped with joy when he heard that the king wanted to see his daughter.

"As soon as the king sees you he'll want to marry you," he said. "Hurry! Be off with you!" And he hustled and bustled his daughter along the road to the palace. At the gates there stood a tall soldier, and the soldier took her into a room full of straw.

The girl looked around, her eyes wide. There was the straw, a spinning-wheel, a wooden stool – but nothing else.

"Ahem," said the tall soldier. "The king says that you are to spin the straw into gold by morning."

"But I can't," said the girl.

The soldier sighed. "Then you will be taken to the dungeons." And he sighed again as he marched away.

The miller's daughter sat down and began to cry. "How can I spin straw into gold?" she sobbed. She cried and cried, until –

CRASH!

The strangest little man burst in through the door – and the door stayed locked behind him.

"Pish! Tush!" he said. "Why are you crying?"

The girl stared. "I have to spin this straw into gold," she said, "and I don't know how!"

"What will you give me if I help you?" asked the little man.

The girl took off her necklace. "Here you are," she said. "Oh – can you really help me?"

"Something for me means something for you," said the little man as he took the necklace and tucked it into his pocket. He sat down and picked up a handful of straw.

R'rrrrm . . . r'rrrrm . . . r'rrrrm . . . the spinning-wheel began to turn.

R'rrrrm . . . r'rrrrm . . . r'rrrrm . . . the little man began to spin the straw.

Faster and faster went the wheel, and the little man hummed as he worked. Louder and softer grew the humming; louder and softer . . . and the miller's daughter shut her eyes and fell fast asleep.

When she woke up it was morning. The strange little man had gone, and so had the straw. There was the spinning-wheel, there was the wooden stool, and – the girl gasped – there was a heap of shining gold.

The king was delighted when the tall soldier came to tell him about the gold.

"Wonderful!" he said. "Wonderful! I shall order my crimson velvet cloak at once. Give the girl food and water, and fill another, larger room with straw. Tell her to spin again tonight. Oh, and tell her if she doesn't she will be thrown into prison forever and ever."

"I'll tell her," said the tall soldier. "But I hope she can do it, if you don't mind my saying so, Your Majesty."

The king rubbed his nose. "Is she pretty?" he asked.

"Yes, sir," said the soldier. "And very hardworking. I could hear the spinning-wheel whirring all night long."

"Ah," said the king. "Splendid!"

That night the miller's daughter sat in the second room full of straw and cried and cried, until –

CRASH!

The strange little man burst in through the door – and the door stayed locked behind him.

"Pish! Tush!" he said. "Crying again?"

"Oh – dear little man – please help me!" said the girl.

"What will you give me?" asked the little man.

The girl pulled her ring off her finger. "It's all I have," she said, and the little man nodded.

"Something for me means something for you," he said, and he sat down and began to spin and to hum. The miller's daughter yawned, and shut her eyes.

When the miller's daughter woke in the morning the little man was gone, but heaps of glistening gold lay all around her.

This time the king was even more delighted. "Splendid! Splendid!" he told the tall soldier. "I shall order my big stone castle today! Tell the girl she must spin one last time. Fill the largest room in the palace with straw, and if she can spin all of it into gold by morning, then I will marry her, and take her to live in my castle. Of course, if she can't—"

"She'll be thrown into prison forever and ever?" suggested the tall soldier.

The king scratched his ear. "Well," he said, "perhaps not forever and ever."

The soldier nodded. "Quite right, sir. She doesn't deserve that."

"No," said the king. "But she might be in prison for quite a long time."

"I'll tell her, sir," said the soldier, and he did.

The miller's daughter sat in the third and largest room and cried and cried, until –

CRASH!

The little man came bursting through the door – and the door stayed locked behind him.

"Pish! Tush!" he said. "Crying again? I can help you!"

The girl shook her head. "It's no good," she said. "I have nothing left to give you."

The little man's eyes shone. "Aha!" he said. "But something for you means something for me!" And he chuckled a wicked little chuckle. "Something for me means something for you – give me a promise, and that will do!"

The girl stared at him. "What do you want me to promise?" she asked.

The little man rubbed his hands together. "Promise that you will give me your first-born baby when you are queen! Promise me that, and I will spin all the straw into gold!"

The girl went on staring at him. When she was queen? A baby? She was so unhappy that she couldn't understand what he was saying. It didn't make any sense to her. But she needed his help, so she nodded her head. "I promise," she said, and the little man cackled with laughter as he flew to the spinning-wheel.

The king married the miller's daughter the very next day. The tall soldier blew his nose hard at the news, but he smiled at the wedding. The miller was as pleased as pleased could be. The girl herself was happy too, for the king was young and handsome. He ordered that everyone in the kingdom was to have their very own cottage and their very own pig, and as soon as his big stone castle was built, the king took the miller's daughter there to live.

It was only when her first baby was born that the miller's daughter thought again about the strange little man.

"Maybe he's forgotten my promise," she said to herself, but all the same she asked the tall soldier to keep careful watch over her son.

It was late one night when the little man slipped through the window – and the window stayed closed behind him. He hopped up to the cradle and peered in, his little black eyes gleaming.

"Something for you means something for me," he said, and he held out his arms for the baby.

"NO!" said the miller's daughter, and she snatched up the baby and held him close. "Please let me keep him! Please!"

The strange little man winked and blinked and laughed his cackling laugh. "I worked for you for three long nights," he said, "so for three nights more the child is yours. But for three nights only. Unless – unless you can guess my name!" Then –

C R A S H ! – he was gone.

The miller's daughter seized a pen and paper and wrote lists and lists of all the names that she could think of. She asked the king and the cook and the miller and the maids. She begged the tall soldier to go out across the kingdom to collect the strangest names he could hear of, and he saddled his horse and rode away.

By the time the sun went down on the first day the miller's daughter was sure that she had found every name ever known. But when the strange little man came hopping through the window, he shook his head all the way from Aaron and Abner to Zachary and Zeus.

The miller's daughter did not give up hope. On the second night she waited for the strange little man with an even longer list, beginning with Apple Blossom and ending with Zubbo. Once again he shook his head at every name.

"Tee hee hee!" he cackled. "Tomorrow the baby will be mine!" And he was still laughing as he disappeared.

The miller's daughter held her baby tightly as she tried and tried to think of a name for the little man. As the sun crawled across the sky she grew more and more frantic, and when at last the tall soldier came limping up the stairs, she ran to meet him.

"Tell me you can save my baby," she said, and she tugged at the soldier's coat. "Please say you can!"

The tall soldier leant against the wall. "I've been North and South and East and West, Your Majesty," he said, "and as I was riding home I passed a deep dark valley. At the bottom was a fire, and dancing round the flames was the strangest little man I've ever seen. He was singing as he danced:

'Something for you means something for me,
and I'll have a something beginning with B.
The baby's mine; I've won the game –
for Rumpelstiltskin is my name!'"

The miller's daughter hugged her baby, and then she hugged the soldier.
"Thank you, thank you!" she said, and she ran up to her room. She hardly had time to put the baby in his cradle before the little man came jumping in through the window.
"Give me the baby!" he said. "Give him to me!"
"Wait," said the miller's daughter, and she sat down. "I still have tonight."
"I'm tired of waiting," said the little man. "Three more guesses, and then no more."
"Very well," said the miller's daughter, and she smiled a little secret smile. "Is your name . . . Twinkletoes?"
"No," said the little man, and he took a step towards the cradle. "Give me the child!"
"I have two more guesses," said the miller's daughter. "Is your name . . . Gobblenuts?"

"NO!" said the little man, and he took another step. "Give me that child! He's MINE!"

"One last guess," said the miller's daughter, and now her heart was beating very fast. "One last guess. Is your name . . .

RUMPELSTILTSKIN?"

The strange little man gave a mighty howl, and he stamped his foot. He was so angry and he stamped so hard that he went straight through the floor –

"OWWWWWWWW!"

– and was never ever seen again.

The miller's daughter bent down and lifted the baby from the cradle. "We're safe now, my little one," she said. "Come see the stars." And she opened the window wide.

Cinderella

TICK TOCK – TICK TOCK – TICK TOCK . . .
Once there was a clock, and the clock was on a tower, and the tower belonged to a white-walled palace. Inside the palace lived a king and a queen and a handsome prince, and outside the palace were all the houses of the kingdom. There were big houses and little houses, small houses and tall houses, and in the tallest house of all lived a girl called Cinderella.

"CINDERELLA!
Cinderella! Cinderella!"
All day long Cinderella ran up
and down the stairs of the
tallest house. All day long she
was busy fetching and
carrying and cooking and
cleaning for her two stepsisters
and her stepmother. All day
long she was washing and
scrubbing and stitching and
sewing, and nobody ever said
please, and nobody ever said
thank you.

When she was little
Cinderella had lived alone
in the tallest house with her
father, and very happy they
were together. Her father
loved his daughter, but he
worried that she was lonely,
and he married again. He
married a woman with two
daughters of her own, Perlina
and Clorinda. Not long
afterwards he died . . .
and at once Cinderella's new
stepmother sent her down
to the kitchen to work.
Perlina and Clorinda took
Cinderella's pretty clothes
and wore them themselves.
Cinderella was left with only
rags and tatters as she sat
among the cinders of the
kitchen fire.

TICK TOCK – TICK TOCK – TICK TOCK . . .
The clock on the palace tower went ticking on. The king and the queen in the palace began to feel old and grey, and they looked at the handsome prince.

"Son, dear Son," said the queen. "Isn't it time that you married?"

The handsome prince bowed. "Of course, dear Mama. But who shall I choose? Sometimes I dream of a beautiful girl, but I've never met her yet."

"We will have a ball in the palace," said the king. "We will have decorations and dancing and delicious things to eat. We will ask all the prettiest girls in the kingdom, and you shall choose a wife."

The handsome prince bowed again. "What a good idea, Papa. But I think we should ask ALL the girls in the kingdom. Sometimes the pretty ones aren't very nice. Besides," – he bowed again – "think how unkind it would be to ask some of the girls and not the others!"

"Quite right, quite right, my dear!" said the queen, who was not very pretty herself.

"Just as you wish, dear boy," said the king.

TICK TOCK – TICK TOCK – TICK TOCK . . .
Time went ticking on, and the invitations were
sent. The girls of the kingdom gazed in
their mirrors and dreamt about dancing
with the handsome prince. In the tallest
house Perlina and Clorinda ran to their
mother to ask what they should wear.

"Green silk for you, Perlina," said the
stepmother, "and for you, Clorinda –
peach satin. Cinderella, you will make
the dresses, and you will sew them with
the neatest of stitches. Isn't that so?"

Cinderella curtsied. "Of course,
Stepmother. But what shall I wear?"

"YOU?" said Perlina. "You in your rags and tatters?"

"YOU?" said Clorinda. "You who sit in the cinders?"

The stepmother smiled. "Dear me, Cinderella. How I wish that you could go to the
ball . . . but – alas – I fear there will be much too much to do! No no, Cinderella. You
will be much too busy preparing the soup and lighting the fires and warming our rooms
ready for our return. Dear me. Such a shame."

Cinderella curtsied again. "Yes, Stepmother," she said, but she sighed as she turned to
go back to the kitchen.

TICK TOCK – TICK TOCK – TICK TOCK . . .

The clock went ticking on. Cinderella
stitched and sewed and cut and
snipped while Perlina and
Clorinda badgered and
bothered her all day long.
They asked for more frills,
and extra buttons, and
different trimming, and
bigger bows. At last even
their mother grew tired and
sent them away to their
rooms.

TICK TOCK – TICK TOCK – TICK TOCK . . .

Time went ticking on until it was the day of the ball. The dresses were finished, and Perlina and Clorinda put them on. They flounced and frolicked round and round the room, and their mother stood and smiled. Cinderella tied their bows and brushed their hair and sighed as she watched them wrapping themselves in their shawls.

"Now, Cinderella," said the stepmother. "Be sure to be ready for us on our return. Fires in every room, remember, and soup hot on the stove."

"That's right," said Perlina. "And you'd better be ready to curtsey, because I shall be chosen to marry the prince."

"YOU?" said Clorinda. "You mean ME!"

"Time to go, my poppets," said the stepmother, and she swept them away to the ball.

TICK TOCK – TICK TOCK – TICK TOCK . . .
The clock went ticking on as Cinderella sat beside her tiny fire in the damp dark kitchen.

"How I wish I could go to the ball," she said, and a tear slowly rolled down her cheek.

WHOOSH! The fire roared up into a blaze of warmth and light.

CLATTER! The dirty cups and plates ran across the table, spun themselves shining clean and leapt onto the shelves.

BUBBLE, BUBBLE, BUBBLE!
The potatoes, onions and peas hopped up and down, stripped off their skins and jumped into the saucepan on the stove.

Cinderella stared and stared.

"Tut, tut," said a croaky little voice. "Don't tell me you've never seen magic before!"

Cinderella turned, and saw a little old woman with twinkling eyes sitting by the fire. The kitchen cat was on her lap, purring loudly.

"Now, my pet," said the little woman. "Did you know you had a fairy godmother?"

Cinderella shook her head.

"Well you do, and here I am. Were you wanting to go to the ball?"

Cinderella could only nod.

"Nothing easier," said the godmother. "Quick, Tabby Cat! Fetch me six mice! And I'd like them alive, if you please. Cinderella, run and pick the pumpkin in the garden. You'll find two lizards just behind the step – bring those too. Hurry along, now!"

In no time at all the mice, the lizards and the pumpkin were in the kitchen. The godmother raised her hand.

"TICKETTY, TOCKETTY, TOO TOO TOO!"
There was a burst of such brightly coloured stars that Cinderella shut her eyes and Tabby Cat hid under the table.

"There we are," said the godmother. "I think that will do very nicely. How pretty you are, my child – I couldn't see it before. All those rags – *most* unbecoming!"

Cinderella opened her eyes . . .

She was dressed in shimmering silk, stars shone in her hair, and her shoes were
starlight-crystal. The kitchen doors opened and outside was a golden coach with
six snow-white horses. A coachman in lizard-green velvet held the reins, and a
footman dressed in the same green velvet bowed to Cinderella.

"Off you go, my pet," said the godmother. "You mustn't keep the prince
waiting!"

"Thank you, THANK YOU," said Cinderella, "Oh, how can I thank you enough?"
And she kissed the little old woman and climbed into the carriage.

"Oh! Oh! Oh!" The fairy godmother ran to the carriage window. "I nearly forgot!
Be sure to leave the palace before midnight! My magic will end as the clock strikes
twelve. Don't forget, now!"

"I'll remember," Cinderella
promised. The coachman
shook the reins, the horses
tossed their heads and
the golden carriage
rattled away to the ball.

TICK TOCK – TICK TOCK – TICK TOCK . . .

The clock went ticking on.

Inside the palace the musicians were playing and the dancers were whirling round and round . . . all except for Perlina and Clorinda. No one had asked them to dance.

"Be patient, my poppets," said their mother. "Your time will come. See! The prince himself is not dancing either!"

The prince was leaning against a pillar and sighing.

"Pretty girls, plain girls, fat girls, thin girls . . . but I don't care for a single one. Will I ever find somebody to love?"

There was a fanfare of trumpets. The prince looked up, and there was Cinderella, in her shimmering dress and her starlight shoes. She saw the prince, and her heart began to dance.

"Oh!" said the prince, and his heart began to sing.

All evening the prince and Cinderella danced together. All evening they looked into each other's eyes, and all evening they smiled at each other alone.

"Who is she?" whispered Perlina.

"She must be a princess," hissed Clorinda.

"It's not fair," they both said together. "It's not fair!"

"Tell me your name," said the prince as he and Cinderella held hands and walked on the balcony. "You are the one I have always dreamed of . . . what is your name?"

Cinderella smiled, but as she turned to the prince she saw the palace clock.

TICK TOCK – TICK TOCK – TICK TOCK . . .
One minute to midnight!

"I must go – I must hurry!" Cinderella said, and she ran and ran, down the stairs, out of the palace, down the steps to the road outside. As she ran the clock struck and struck . . . and the coach shrivelled . . . and the horses shrank . . . and the coachman and the footman whisked away under the bushes.

At the last stroke of midnight all that was left was the pumpkin lying at the side of the road. Cinderella shivered as she ran, her rags fluttering about her.

"Stop! Stop!" The prince came dashing down the stairs. As he leapt from step to step something glittered and caught his eye. He picked it up and found it was Cinderella's shoe. There was nothing else. No princess, nothing.

"I will find her," said the prince. "I will send messengers far and wide! I will only ever marry the girl whose foot fits this shoe . . . I will marry her and no other." And he went back to the palace to tell the king and the queen.

Perlina and Clorinda were not at all pleased when they came back from the ball. They grumbled and moaned, and would not eat the soup that Cinderella brought them.

"I wanted chicken broth," said Perlina.

"And I wanted barley!" said Clorinda.

"Time for my poppets to go to bed," said their mother.

TICK TOCK – TICK TOCK – TICK TOCK . . .

The clock ticked the night away.

The very next morning a messenger came knocking on the door of the tallest house.

"All who went to the ball are to try on the crystal shoe!" he announced. "The prince will marry the girl whose foot it fits!" He snapped his fingers and a pageboy came in carrying the crystal shoe on a velvet cushion. Behind the pageboy came the prime minister, and behind the prime minister marched four fine soldiers.

"It's MY shoe!" said Perlina.

"No! It's MINE!" said Clorinda, and they snatched at the shoe together.

"Ahem," said the prime minister. "One at a time, dear ladies, if you please."

"LOOK!" said Perlina, and she balanced the tiny shoe on her toes. "It fits!"

"No!" said Clorinda, and she squeezed the shoe over her heel. "It's MINE!"

"Ahem," said the prime minister. "I don't think so. No." And he put the shoe back on the cushion with a sigh of relief. "Are there any other young ladies?"

"NO!" said Perlina and Clorinda.

"Certainly not!" said their mother.

"Excuse me, but might I try on the slipper?"

Perlina, Clorinda and their mother gasped and glared as Cinderella stepped into the room.

"YOU?" said Perlina.

"What are YOU doing here?" asked Clorinda.

"Cinderella," said the stepmother, "go straight back down to the kitchen." She turned to the prime minister. "Poor girl. She dreams. Of course she was never at the ball."

"But I was," said Cinderella, and she took the glittering glass shoe from the cushion and slipped it onto her foot. It fitted, exactly.

The prime minister's eyes opened wide. The pageboy stared. The soldiers gawped. Perlina and Clorinda clutched at their mother's arm.

"And here's the other shoe," said Cinderella, and she took it out of her apron pocket.

"SOUND THE TRUMPETS!" called the prime minister. "THE PRINCESS IS FOUND!"

"Indeed she is," said a voice – and there beside Cinderella was the fairy godmother. "But we can't have her wearing such rags and tatters. Oh dear me, no. TICKETTY TOCKETTY TOO!"

She waved her wand . . . then disappeared in a shower of golden stars.

Cinderella was dressed in a dress of golden satin, shining like the sun. As the prince came hurrying through the door, she curtsied to her stepmother and her stepsisters.

"I wish you all well," she said, "for my father's sake." Then she took the prince's hand and rode away to the white-walled palace, and there they both lived happily ever after.

TICK TOCK – TICK TOCK – TICK TOCK . . .